This book belongs to

Bluebell Glade

Dandelion Dell

Heart of Misty Woo

Hawthorn Hedgerows

How many Fairy Animals books have you collected?

- Chloe the Kitten
- Bella the Bunny
- Paddy the Puppy
- Mia the Mouse
- Poppy the Pony
- Hailey the Hedgehog
- ✓ Sophie the Squirrel
- Daisy the Deer

And there are more magical adventures coming very soon!

Fairy Animals

of Misty Wood

Sophie the Squirrel

Lily Small

Henry Holt and Company
New York

With special thanks to Gill Harvey

Henry Holt and Company
Publishers since 1866
175 Fifth Avenue
New York, New York 10010
mackids.com

First published in the United States in 2017 by Henry Holt and Company.
Originally published in Great Britain in 2014 by Egmont UK Limited.

Library of Congress Cataloging-in-Publication Data is available.
ISBN 978-1-62779-740-5

Our books may be purchased in bulk for promotional, educational, or business use.
Please contact your local bookseller or the Macmillan Corporate
and Premium Sales Department at (800) 221-7945 ext. 5442
or by e-mail at MacmillanSpecialMarkets@macmillan.com.

First American Edition—2017
Printed in the United States of America by
LSC Communications US, LLC (Lakeside Classic), Harrisonburg, Virginia

3 5 7 9 10 8 6 4 2

Contents

CHAPTER ONE

Rise and Shine!

Misty Wood was brimming over
with excitement. The sun was
beaming happily as he stretched
his rays out to every corner of the

1

wood. The leaves on the trees were rustling cheerfully. The blooms in the meadows were bobbing their heads joyfully in the breeze. And everywhere you looked, fairy animals were fluttering their sparkling wings and whispering behind their paws.

"Tomorrow is the fair!" they chattered. "Tomorrow is the *fair*!"

High up in an old oak tree, a pretty little face popped out of

2

a hole in the trunk. The face was followed by a silky red body with sparkly violet wings. Last of all came a bushy golden tail that twitched to and fro. It was Sophie the Stardust Squirrel.

"Tomorrow is going to be the best day of my whole life!" she cried. "I can't wait, I can't wait!" Sophie was especially excited because she and her friends had been chosen to perform the opening

dance at the Misty Wood fair
this year.

Sophie hopped onto a branch
and smoothed down her whiskers.
Then she flexed her fairy wings
and closed her eyes, imagining
what tomorrow would be like.

The opening dance of the Misty
Wood fair was always lovely. Every
year, some clever Bark Badgers
made a wooden festival pole, carved
with woodland scenes and beautiful

swirling patterns. It was placed in the middle of a big, grassy clearing, then brightly colored strands of flowers were attached like ribbons to stream down from the top. Each dancer held a strand and skipped around the pole.

Today the pole would finally be ready, and Sophie and her friends would get the chance to have one last practice.

Sophie jiggled her tail at the

very thought and scampered down the old oak tree. She was so excited, she couldn't stay still! When she reached the bottom, she jumped back up again, imagining that the tree was the pole. As she twisted and turned around the gnarled trunk, she thought of all the other fairy animals, cheering loudly as she and her friends performed the dance.

Just as she reached the top of the tree, she heard someone shouting.

7

"What's all that scraping and scuffling?" Sophie's mom called.

Sophie peered down through the branches. Her mom was poking her head out of the nest in the cozy hollow where they lived, looking this way and that.

"It's only me, Mom," Sophie replied.

"Sophie! Whatever are you up to?" asked her mom, looking up at her. "You're making so much noise that you woke poor Sammy from his nap."

"Oh, I'm sorry, Mom!" Sophie exclaimed. Sammy was Sophie's little brother. He was still very young, so he always had a midday snooze. "I didn't mean to wake him. I'm just so excited about tomorrow."

Sophie's mom smiled. "Yes, I understand. I remember dancing at the fair when I was your age. It was so much fun. But try not to get *too* excited, Sophie—look at what you've done to our tree!"

10

"Done? I haven't done anything . . ." Sophie began. But as she looked around the branches, she clapped her paw to her mouth. The old oak tree was shimmering silver from head to foot! The leaves were no longer green. The trunk was no longer brown. Every single part of the tree was covered in stardust!

Like all the other fairy animals in Misty Wood, Stardust Squirrels

had their own special job. Their
big, bushy tails sprinkled stardust
whenever the squirrels gave them
a shake. They were supposed to
scatter the dust lightly over Misty
Wood so that it twinkled gently. But
the oak tree wasn't just twinkling
now. It was *glowing*!

"Never mind," chuckled
Sophie's mom. "The next time it
rains it will all get washed away.
And, in the meantime, it's quite

nice having the brightest tree in the
whole wood—at least we'll be able
to find our way home in the dark!
Now it's time you went to your
practice."

"Oh! Is it?" Sophie sat up on
her back legs and wiggled her
whiskers.

Sophie's mom nodded.

"Hurray!" cheered Sophie.
"We're going to dance around
the festival pole at last!" With

two enormous flicks of her tail, she bounded down the tree, scattering more stardust. She looked up at her mom to wave good-bye. "Uh-oh . . ." she murmured.

Her mom's head had turned silver now, too. It was hard to tell where she ended and the tree began!

Sophie's mom laughed and gave her head a shake, sending a cloud of stardust shimmering to the ground.

"Good luck," she called. "And be careful what you do with that tail!"

"I will," Sophie said with a grin. "See you later, Mom." And with a flutter of her fairy wings, she flew off to find her friends.

CHAPTER TWO

Practice Makes Perfect

Sophie rose up above the trees,
enjoying the feel of the breeze
ruffling her soft fur.

First of all she had to fetch

her friend Katie from Hawthorn
Hedgerows.

It was a beautiful sunny day,
and the delicious scent of hawthorn
blossoms wafted toward Sophie as
she swooped over the hedges. Soon

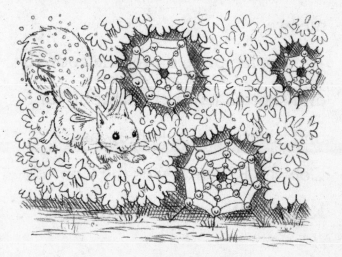

the glint of a shiny dewdrop caught her eye, and she dived down to land near a silvery cobweb.

"Katie!" she called. "Where are you?"

"I'm over here!" a tinkly voice meowed.

Sophie peeked over the cobweb and spotted her friend's tabby fur and silvery wings. Katie was a Cobweb Kitten. It was the Cobweb Kittens' job to collect dewdrops

every morning from Dewdrop

Spring, then use them to decorate

the cobwebs in Misty Wood.

Sophie watched as Katie fished

a dewdrop from her little basket and

balanced it perfectly on one of the cobweb's delicate threads.

"Almost finished!" said Katie. "Only two more to go!"

"Good," said Sophie. "It's time for our final dance practice."

"I know," Katie purred. "I was so excited this morning, I kept dropping my dewdrops! That's why I haven't quite finished yet."

"I can help you," Sophie offered. "Shall we place one each?"

20

Katie gave a big smile. "Yes, please!" She pointed a snowy white paw to the top of a nearby hedge. "Could you put one on that tiny cobweb over there?"

Sophie nodded eagerly. Then she bounded forward and scooped a dewdrop from Katie's basket. It glimmered like a precious diamond in her paws. Holding it carefully, she carried it over to the cobweb. She felt honored to be helping

21

Katie do her job. Sophie placed the dewdrop on the silky strand of web and hopped back.

"Ooh, thank you, Sophie—that looks lovely," Katie said.

Sophie turned to Katie and smiled. "Come on, then, let's go and get Bonnie."

The two friends fluttered off toward Honeydew Meadow. Bonnie was a Bud Bunny. The Bud Bunnies' special job was to nudge

the flower buds into bloom by twitching their noses against them. Now, thanks to their hard work, the meadow was bursting with all the colors of the rainbow.

Sophie and Katie hovered over the sea of color for a moment, looking for their friend. Then, in the middle of a patch of pale blue flowers, Sophie spotted Bonnie's sparkly pink wings and soft white fur.

"There she is!" Sophie cried.
"She's just about to open another
flower."

Bonnie was sitting perfectly

24

still with her nose very close to a nodding flower bud. As Sophie and Katie watched, Bonnie's nose twitched . . . and one by one, the petals of the flower burst open.

Sophie and Katie flew down to land beside Bonnie, clapping their paws. Bonnie's long white ears pricked up at the sight of her two friends.

"Hi, Bonnie! Your flowers are so pretty," Sophie said. "Are

you ready to come to our dance practice?"

Bonnie twirled her whiskers. "Ooh, is it time?" she asked.

Sophie and Katie nodded.

"I'd better just tell my mom. She's working over there," said Bonnie, waving her paw in the direction of some brightly colored tulips.

Bonnie's mom was sitting in the middle of the tulips, twitching

her nose against one of the glossy buds. The friends scampered up to her just as the tulip burst into bloom. Its petals were as yellow and shiny as the sun.

"Mom, can I go to my dance practice?" Bonnie asked.

"Of course." Bonnie's mom smiled at the little fairy animals, and her fluffy cotton tail began thumping on the ground. "I have a nice surprise for you, too."

27

"Ooh, I love surprises!" Sophie exclaimed, and her tail twitched, sending a puff of stardust into the air.

"What kind of surprise is it?" Bonnie asked, hopping around to catch some stardust on the tips of her ears.

Bonnie's mom smoothed back her whiskers and leaned toward them. "I'm going to make each of you a flower garland to wear when

you do your dance at the fair," she said. "I'm going to use the prettiest flowers in all of Misty Wood's meadows!"

Sophie was so pleased, her wings started fluttering. As she rose into the air, her tail twitched this way and that, showering stardust all over the tulips.

"Thank you!" she cried.

"Thank you!" Bonnie and Katie chorused.

"You're welcome," Bonnie's mom said with a smile.

"Now we just have to go and get Polly," Sophie said.

"Have fun!" Bonnie's mom called as she hopped over to a big cluster of crimson poppy buds and began nudging them open.

Sophie, Katie, and Bonnie swooped away, heading toward Dandelion Dell. It wasn't very far, and soon they could see golden

dandelions spread out like a carpet of sunshine below them.

The Pollen Puppies were hard at work, bouncing from one patch of blooms to another, wagging their tails as they went. They were doing a very important job—with each wag of their tails, they spread pollen so that there would be even more dandelions next year.

The three friends fluttered around in circles, looking for Polly.

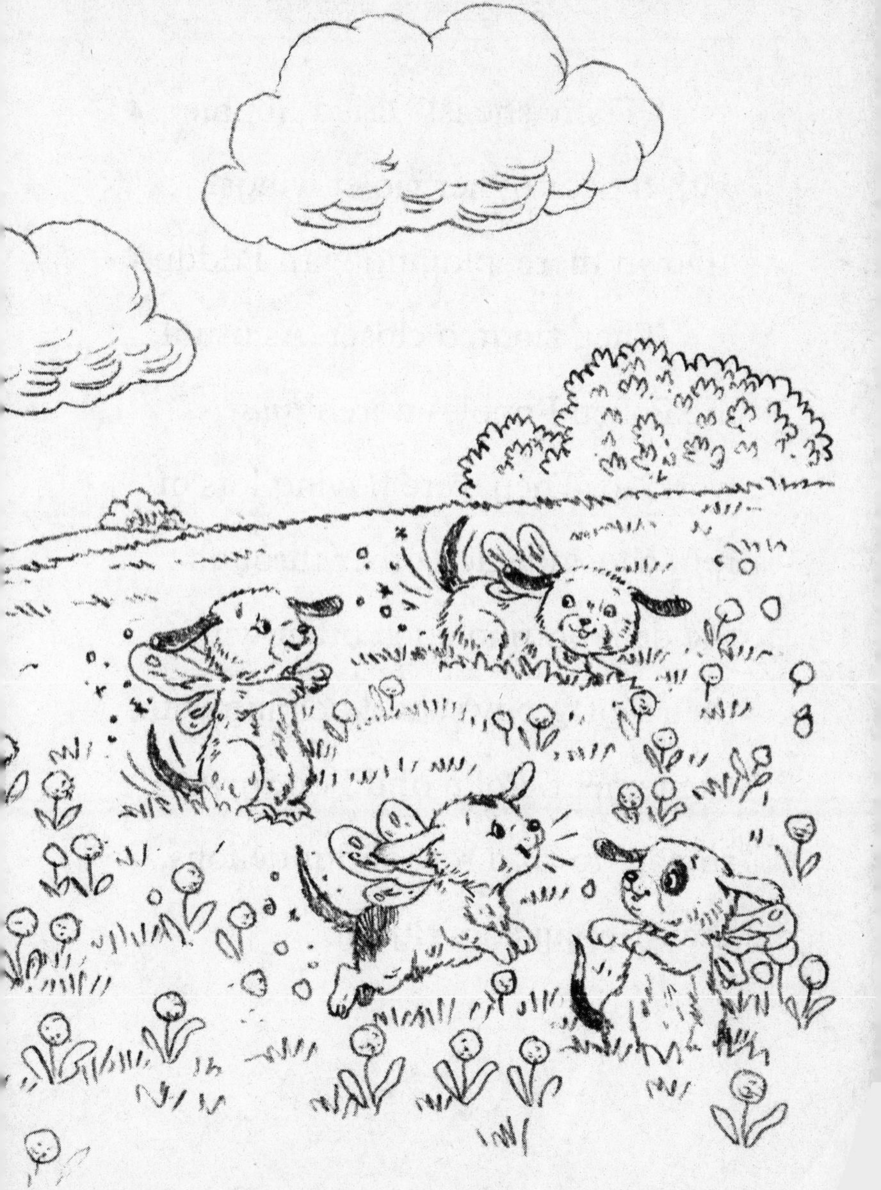

"There she is!" cried Sophie with a beat of her violet wings. "Down there, playing with Paddy."

They floated closer. As usual, the Pollen Puppies weren't *just* working. They were having lots of fun, chasing each other through the dell, batting each other with their fluffy paws, and yelping with excitement. Polly and Paddy were racing down a row of dandelions, their floppy ears flying.

"Polly!" called Katie, fluttering down to land. "It's time for our last dance practice."

Polly skidded to a halt next to a tall, tufty dandelion. "Oh!" she cried. "Is it really?" She clapped her paws, and her coppery brown tail wagged harder than ever.

Sophie, Katie, and Bonnie gathered around.

"Sorry, Paddy," said Polly. "I have to go now. Do you think

you can finish the rest on your own?"

"Of course!" Paddy panted, his little pink tongue hanging out. "But first I'm going to race my tail."

"How do you race your own tail?" Sophie asked with a frown.

"Easy peasy," Paddy replied. "Look!" And with that, he bounded off, his tail wagging so fast it became a golden blur.

Polly smoothed down her ears and rustled her golden wings. "I'm ready," she told the others. "Let's go!"

Sophie, Katie, Bonnie, and Polly flew off across the dell and

into the Heart of Misty Wood.
As they soared through the trees,
Sophie's wings flapped faster and
faster—she couldn't wait to see the
festival pole. But when they got to
the clearing where the dance was
supposed to take place, there was
no pole to be seen.

They fluttered down to the
ground and looked around. An old
Bark Badger with silvery wings was
busy carving beautiful patterns

into the bark of a nearby tree. They scampered over to him.

"Excuse me," Sophie said. "Do you know where the festival pole is? We've been chosen to perform the opening dance at the fair tomorrow, and we need to practice."

The badger stopped what he was doing and smiled at Sophie. "I'm sorry, little Stardust Squirrel, but the pole isn't quite ready yet," he said. "My badger friends are

sick, so I am decorating it all on my own. It won't be ready until tomorrow morning."

"But the fair starts in the morning!" Sophie gasped.

The four friends looked at one another. They had worked out all their steps. They'd gone through them so many times that they knew them by heart. But they'd never practiced with ribbons and a pole. What were they going to do?

40

CHAPTER THREE
Hello, Mr. Bluebird!

Sophie rubbed her nose with her paw. "We'll have to find a different kind of pole," she said, "and pretend that it's the proper one."

41

"Yes," Katie agreed. "There has to be something that will do, somewhere in Misty Wood."

They sat in a huddle and tried to think. What would be tall and strong and ribbony enough to make a good practice pole? They scratched their heads and tugged their whiskers. But it was no use— they couldn't think of anything.

"Maybe we should just go and look for one," Sophie said at last.

"Yes," said Bonnie. "But we'll have to be quick. We'll never be ready by tomorrow if we don't find one soon!"

They unfurled their wings and flew off together to begin the hunt. They soared over Hawthorn Hedgerows, but there were only twigs and bushes there. Then they made for Honeydew Meadow, but they could see only pretty flowers.

Next, they glided around the

Heart of Misty Wood, but the trees there were too tall and tangly. When they flew over Moonshine Pond, they saw lots of dragonflies, but they didn't see anything that looked like a good practice pole.

"What are we going to *do*?" wailed Katie, her tabby tail drooping.

"Let's try Dewdrop Spring," Sophie said.

"But that's just water," said

Katie sadly. "I've never seen anything like a pole there."

Sophie knew that her friend was probably right. But they couldn't give up—not until they had searched all of Misty Wood. As they fluttered toward Dewdrop Spring, Sophie spotted something in the distance that made her heart leap.

"Look!" she exclaimed, pointing down. "It's perfect!"

There, on the bank of the

spring, stood an elegant willow tree. Its trunk was tall and straight, but its thin branches swept down all around it—just like ribbons.

"Oh yes, of course," purred Katie happily. "Well done, Sophie!"

"Hurray!" cried Bonnie.

Polly yapped gleefully and did a loop-the-loop, then zoomed down to the willow tree at full speed. Giggling and chattering, the other three followed her. They skipped

around the tree, deciding which branches would make the best ribbons.

Suddenly, they heard a voice.

"What's all that noise around my tree?" it twittered.

The four friends fell silent at once. They squinted up into the willow tree.

"It's only . . . only . . . us . . ." Sophie began, peering through the branches. She couldn't see anything

at first, but then, right at the top

of the tree, she spied a little nest.

And perched on the nest was a

bluebird, with feathers the color of

a bright summer sky.

"We're sorry, Mr. Bluebird," Sophie said. "It's the Misty Wood fair tomorrow, and we're performing the opening dance—but we don't have a pole to practice with. Your tree is the only thing we've found. Would you mind if we use it, just for a little while?"

The bluebird hopped out of his nest and flew down to the ground.

"The opening dance, eh?" he chirped, tilting his head.

"Yes," Sophie said, nodding.

"That sounds very important," tweeted the bluebird. "Important enough for you to use my tree. But won't you need some music to dance to?"

"Oh yes," said Bonnie. "We'll have music tomorrow. The Moss Mouse band will be playing for us while we dance."

"But what about now?" asked the bluebird. "How are you going

to practice if you don't have any music *now*?"

Sophie, Katie, Bonnie, and Polly looked at each other. The bluebird was right. They couldn't *really* know how the dance would go if they'd never tried it with music.

"Well . . ." said Sophie slowly, twitching her whiskers. She was beginning to feel a bit nervous. "I suppose we'll just have to hope for the best."

52

"No, no, no," chirped the bluebird, shaking his head. "That won't do at all. You *must* practice with music. And I know exactly what music you should have."

"You do?" Polly looked at him hopefully and her tail began to wag.

"It just so happens that I'm one of the best singers in the whole of Misty Wood," said the bluebird proudly. "So, as you've come to *my* tree and want to dance under *my*

53

nest, I think I should help the four of you out."

"Really?" Sophie gasped. "You'll sing for us?"

The bluebird puffed out his feathery chest. "I certainly will. Are you ready?"

Fumbling in excitement, the friends scampered around the tree, quickly deciding on which willow branches to use. When each of them was holding a branch, the bluebird

spread his wings, threw back his head, and began to sing in a sweet, soaring voice.

It was the most beautiful song that any of them had ever heard. They danced in time, weaving in and out of one another around the tree. First one way, then another, and then . . .

"Ow!" cried Sophie, stopping with a bump.

The bluebird stopped singing

and flew over to her. "What is it, little squirrel?" he asked.

"It's my tail," gasped Sophie. "I can't move it!"

Sophie's friends gathered around.

"It's all tangled up in the branches," Katie meowed.

Sophie pulled her tail one way. Then she pulled it the other way. But it was no use. She was well and truly stuck!

HELLO, MR. BLUEBIRD!

CHAPTER FOUR

Triple Trouble

"Oh no!" Sophie cried. "How can we practice for the dance if I'm stuck to the tree?" She looked at her friends, her brown eyes widened

in fear. "What if I'm stuck here forever?"

"Don't worry." Bonnie hopped over and patted Sophie with her paw. "We'll soon figure it out."

"We just need to be patient," Katie agreed. "We'll untangle it one branch at a time."

"I'll sing you a patient song, if you like," the little bluebird chirped, perching himself on a branch in

front of Sophie. He began tweeting very slowly and gently.

Polly, Bonny, and Katie began working on Sophie's tail. Slowly and gently, in time with the song, they untwisted the long, thin willow branches one by one. Sophie watched them anxiously over her shoulder. Sometimes they accidentally pulled her fur, and she had to try hard not to yelp. To take her mind off it, she closed her

60

eyes and thought of yummy acorns instead.

Just as Sophie was thinking of her twenty-second acorn, Polly clapped her paws.

"You're free!" she woofed.

Sophie opened her eyes. The

bluebird was flying around and around in a circle, chirping wildly.

Sophie hopped forward. It felt so good to be able to move again. "Thank you!" she exclaimed in relief. "And don't worry, I'll be doubly careful with my tail from now on!"

They all took their positions around the tree, and the bluebird flew up to the top.

"All ready?" he called down.

"Yes!" they chorused.

He opened his little beak and began his beautiful song again. The dance started, and soon Sophie had forgotten all about trapping her tail. As she and her friends skipped in time with the bluebird's melody she felt herself getting more and more excited.

Tomorrow is going to be so wonderful, Sophie thought to herself. *It's going to be the best day of my—*

"*AAAHHH . . . CHOO!*"

Sophie jumped as a loud sneeze rang out across the banks of the spring. Then it got even worse.

"*AAAHHH . . . CHOO! Cough, cough, COUGH!*"

Sophie stopped dancing and looked around. Bonnie was doubled over behind her. Her floppy ears were lying flat and her pink eyes were streaming.

"Oh no!" gulped Sophie.

64

She could see at once what the problem was. Bonnie's normally snowy white fur was glimmering silver. Sophie had gotten so excited while she'd been dancing that she'd showered Bonnie in stardust!

"*Cough cough cough*," spluttered Bonnie. "I've got stardust up my— *aaahhh . . . choo*—nose."

"I'm so sorry," cried Sophie. "Oh dear, my tail's causing all sorts of problems today."

65

Polly let go of her branch and bounded over. "Don't worry," she yapped. "I'll soon fix it."

She scampered around Bonnie, wagging her tail, just as she did when she was flicking pollen in the meadows. *Flick flick flick*, went her tail. *Flick flick flickety flick* . . .

Bonnie started to giggle. "It tickles!" she cried as Polly's tail flicked away at her fur.

The bluebird flew above them,

67

chirping jauntily, and soon Polly had flicked all the stardust away.

"Oh, well done, Polly!" Sophie exclaimed. "You've done a really great job!"

"Yes, thanks, Polly," agreed Bonnie, wiping her eyes dry. "I'm ready to start dancing again."

"Right," said Sophie. "And *this* time my tail won't cause any problems. I won't let it!"

So off around the tree they

68

went. Sophie concentrated really hard. She mustn't shake her tail too much, and she mustn't get it stuck.

"I'll tuck it between my legs," she muttered to herself.

As the practice went on, Sophie began to feel happier and more confident. With her tail tucked tightly between her legs, there were no more problems. But just as they whirled around the tree

one last time, Sophie suddenly felt herself hurtling forward.

"Wahhhhhh!" she cried.

THUMP. She fell flat on her face.

"Help!" squeaked Bonnie, bumping into Sophie.

"Uh-oh!" yelped Polly, landing on Bonnie's back.

"Oh no!" meowed Katie, falling head over heels on top of them all!

"Oh no, oh no, oh no!" the

bluebird tweeted as he hovered

above.

The four fairy animals lay in

a heap on the ground, their paws,

wings, and tails in a higgledy-piggledy jumble. Sophie lay at the bottom of the pile, trying to work out what had happened. And then she realized. She'd tucked her tail so tightly between her legs that she'd tripped right over it!

A big, fat tear rolled down Sophie's cheek. "It's all my fault," she wept. "Everything's going wrong, and I'll never be able to get the dance right. *Never!*"

CHAPTER FIVE

Shooting Star!

A delicious smell wafted through
the cozy hollow in the old oak tree.
It was Sophie's favorite dinner—
acorn soup—and her dad had just

finished making it. But Sophie didn't feel hungry at all. Her baby brother banged his wooden spoon and gurgled impatiently, but Sophie was quite sure that she wouldn't be able to eat even the tiniest bit. She sat on her little sycamore stool in the corner, feeling glum.

"What's the matter?" Sophie's mom asked. "Didn't your practice go well?"

Sophie shook her head. "No,

it didn't." She could feel her lip beginning to wobble.

"Oh, never mind," her dad said with a smile. "It can't have been that bad."

"But it *was*," Sophie cried. "Everyone's going to laugh at me at the fair. I can't dance at all!"

"Yes you can," said her dad. "You're a lovely dancer."

"Not anymore," Sophie said, her head drooping low.

Sophie's mom hopped over and stroked her silky fur. "What happened?"

"My tail spoiled everything," Sophie muttered. "First I got it stuck. Then it showered stardust all over Bonnie and made her cough and sneeze. And then I tripped over it—and everyone else tripped over me! Stupid tail!"

"Oh, dear," said Sophie's mom. She wrapped her own bushy tail

around Sophie in a big hug. "But try not to get too upset. Things always go wrong in rehearsals—I'm sure it will be fine at the fair."

Normally, her mom's hugs made Sophie feel a lot better. But not today. All she could think about was how terrible the dance was going to be. She started to cry, and buried her face in her paws.

"It's going . . . to be . . . awful," she sobbed.

"Now, don't you worry," her dad said, giving her one of his twinkly-eyed smiles. "I think I have an idea."

"You do?" Sophie peeked hopefully at him through her paws.

Sophie's dad whispered in her mom's ear, and her mom nodded, her eyes sparkling.

"Oh yes," her mom said in a mysterious voice. "That will work. Definitely!"

Sophie's dad winked at Sophie and beckoned to her. "Come on," he said. "You and I are going out."

"What . . . *now*?" It was dark

outside, and Sophie hardly ever went out at night.

Her dad nodded and held out his paw. "Follow me," he said.

Sophie felt a tiny bit nervous at first, going out in the dark, but she knew she was safe with her dad. He opened his strong red wings and led her up, up, up toward the glowing, pearly face of the moon.

Soon they were high above the

treetops, with nothing but twinkling stars around them. Sophie looked down and gasped. Misty Wood lay out like a map below her—it looked very beautiful in the moonlight. There were the flower buds in the meadows, drooping their little heads as they slept. There were the shimmering waters of Dewdrop Spring. Then Sophie saw flashes of pale light and pointed down excitedly.

"Look, Dad!" she cried.

The Moonbeam Moles were flitting through the darkness below them like shadows, catching glowing moonbeams to drop into Moonshine Pond. Sophie's dad nodded, then carried on flying upward. Sophie had to flap her wings very hard to be able to keep up with him.

"Why are we going so high?" she panted.

Her dad looked back at her and smiled. "It's just a little bit farther."

Sophie fluttered up next to him, panting from all the effort.

"This is what we've come for," her dad explained. "Look. Up there."

Sophie looked. Above her head, the most beautiful shooting star flew past, leaving a rainbow-colored trail of stardust behind it.

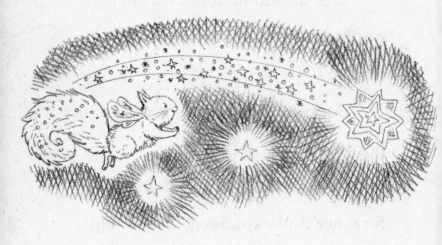

"Wow!" Sophie breathed.

"Now, be quick," her dad said.

"Fly after it and catch some of that
stardust in your tail."

Sophie twitched her bushy tail excitedly. All of a sudden she didn't feel tired at all. The star was the most lovely thing she'd ever seen! She whooshed after it.

The star danced across the sky, making wonderful patterns as it went. Sometimes it zigzagged or soared in spiraling circles. Sometimes it even made the shape of flower petals as it looped around the shining moon.

As Sophie chased the star, she twisted her tail this way and that to catch as much stardust as she could. She completely forgot all her worries about the dance practice. She even forgot about the fair. All she could think about was how happy she was to be out catching rainbow-colored stardust in her fluffy tail.

The shooting star did one last enormous loop, then it disappeared

behind the moon. Sophie gazed after it. Had it really gone? She felt a bit sad. Her dad flew up and placed his paw on her shoulder.

"Shooting stars never last long," he said, "and you did very well to catch so much stardust. You see, shooting-star dust is special."

"Really?" Sophie's eyes shone.

"Yes." Her dad smiled. "It is magical, and now that dust from a shooting star is in your tail, you'll

be able to get it to behave perfectly in the dance tomorrow."

Sophie twitched her ears in disbelief. "Really?"

"Really and truly." Her dad nodded solemnly. "As long as you believe in the magic . . ."

CHAPTER SIX
The Big Day

Dawn was breaking over Misty Wood, spreading pale golden light across the hedgerows and hills, meadows and valleys.

Sophie opened her eyes. She gazed up at the cluster of oak leaves that dangled over her mossy bed, and frowned. A strange memory was taking shape in her head—or had it been a dream? Something about chasing a shooting star . . .

Sophie hopped out of bed and gave her tail a little shake. A puff of rainbow-colored stardust filled the air and drifted down onto her

soft pillow. Sophie gasped. It hadn't

been a dream at all!

Sophie scampered across the cozy hollow to join her mom, her dad, and Sammy at their breakfast table made from polished conkers.

"Good morning, Sophie," said her mom. "Come and have some porridge. You're going to need plenty of energy today!"

Sophie sat down and took a mouthful of porridge. She knew she had to eat, but she was starting to feel nervous. Was her dad right

about the shooting-star dust? Would her tail really be okay?

Sophie had eaten half her porridge when she heard excited chatter coming from outside.

"Sophie, are you ready?" she heard Polly yap.

"It's time to go," Katie meowed.

"It's almost time for the fair!" Bonnie called.

Sophie leaped up from the table, her tail twitching. A cloud of

the special stardust shimmered into the bowls of porridge, like rainbow-colored sugar.

"Whoops!" Sophie exclaimed.

"Yay!" Sammy cried, looking at the porridge with glee.

"Good luck," Sophie's dad said as Bonnie's, Katie's, and Polly's noses peeped into the hollow. "We'll see you there. And don't forget what I told you!" he added with a wink at Sophie.

"I won't," promised Sophie.

She took a deep breath and headed out to join her friends.

Buzzing with energy, the four friends spread their wings and flew out between the trees. It was still early, but lots of fairy animals were already busy, bustling about making preparations for the fair.

Sophie spotted Old Frannie the Fern Fox's tent, draped in garlands of copper beech leaves, where she

would sit telling fairy fortunes all day. Just beyond that, Sophie saw the Misty Wood bees hard at work, building their fairground honeycomb maze. Sophie loved wandering around in the maze, giggling with her friends as they got lost in its endless twists and turns.

As they got closer to the Heart of Misty Wood, Katie pointed at the shimmering, swaying cobweb tent, made from the silky threads

of hundreds of Misty Wood spiders.
Inside the tent would be all sorts of
stalls displaying the fairy animals'
favorite treats.

Every year there was a *Guess
How Many Blackberries* competition.
There would be a cake stall laden
with mounds of hazelnut cakes
and honey buns, acorn pies and
conker crunchies. Flowers from
the meadows would brighten every
corner and, once the Cobweb

97

Maze

fairy fortunes

conker crunch

Honey buns

Guess How many Blackberries

Kittens had gotten to work, the whole tent would be glistening with dewdrops from Dewdrop Spring!

Sophie couldn't wait for the fair to begin. It was all going to be so much fun!

They flew on toward the clearing where the grand opening was to take place. Sophie remembered that before they could explore any of the treats that the fair had in store, they had to

perform their dance. She started feeling a little nervous again. . . .

Down below, in the clearing, Sophie could see some Bark Badgers. They were gathered in a huddle, their silvery wings folded neatly over their striped black-and-white backs. They seemed to be having some kind of urgent meeting. Sophie suddenly felt worried. She couldn't see the festival pole anywhere. Where was

it? Shouldn't the badgers have put it in place by now?

Sophie and her friends fluttered down and scampered over to the badgers. "We're here!" Sophie cried. "We're ready to do our dance."

The badgers turned to them, their faces sad. Sophie's heart thudded. Now she knew for sure that something was wrong.

"Where's the festival pole?" she asked.

The badgers parted so that the four friends could see what they had been gathered around. There, on the vivid green grass, lay the festival pole covered in amazing carvings, with ribbons of flowers streaming from one end. Sophie's eyes shone when she saw how beautiful it was.

But then she noticed something. There was a problem. A *big* problem. The pole was broken in two, right in the middle.

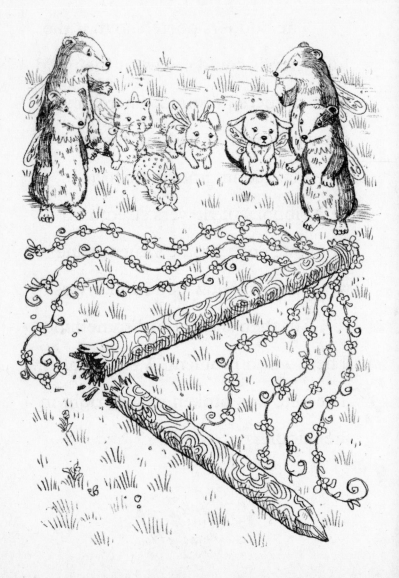

"We just finished decorating it, but it was so heavy we dropped it," explained the badger they had met yesterday. He gave a long, sad sigh. "We're very, very sorry."

Sophie couldn't believe it. She blinked hard, hoping she might see something different when she opened her eyes—but the festival pole was still broken.

"So . . . what should we do now?" she asked in a very small voice.

"Well . . ." The badger stroked his chin and shuffled from one paw to the other. He looked very upset. "I'm afraid that there's nothing we can do. I'm very sorry, but the dance will just have to be canceled."

CHAPTER SEVEN

Rainbow Bright!

Canceled! Sophie rubbed her ears
with her paws, hoping she had
misheard.

The sun was peeping through

the trees around the clearing, and crowds of fairy animals had started to arrive. Over to one side, the Moss Mouse band had begun to play. There was no time left.

A tear rolled down Sophie's cheek. She sat down next to Polly, Bonnie, and Katie. They were all too sad to say anything. The other fairy animals who had begun to gather to watch the dance looked at them curiously.

Sophie thought about how wonderful everything had seemed last night, flying high in the dark sky, chasing the shooting star. She thought of practicing around the willow tree and how her dad had promised that the magical rainbow stardust would make her tail behave. None of that mattered anymore.

But as Sophie remembered all that had happened the day before,

an idea began to form in her mind.
She scrubbed her tears away and
leaped to her feet.

"I know what we're going to do!"
she called. "Everyone follow me!"

Polly's, Bonnie's, and Katie's

eyes widened, and they jumped
up excitedly.

"Where are we going?" asked
Katie.

"You'll soon find out," said
Sophie. "Come on, everyone!" she

called again to all the other fairy animals.

Sophie set off, half scampering, half fluttering, checking over her shoulder that everyone was following. Around the honeycomb maze, past the cobweb tent—she hurried on until she reached the banks of Dewdrop Spring.

The willow tree stood there, its branches draping down to the ground. Sophie bounded up to it.

She gave a shake of her tail, and
a little cloud of rainbow-colored
stardust puffed out. Then she flew
up and around the tree, shaking her
tail until the whole willow glittered
with glorious colors. Soon its trunk
glowed red, orange, and yellow,
and its branches looked like green,
purple, pink, and blue ribbons—
only even prettier!

"Wow!" gasped Katie, Bonnie,
and Polly as Sophie flew back.

"How did you do that?" Polly woofed, her tail wagging wildly. "It looks *beautiful*!"

"It's magic," Sophie said with a grin.

The fairy animals that had followed them began to flutter about, chattering to one another and spreading the news: The dance was back on! The Bark Badgers looked very relieved indeed.

As the crowd began to grow,

the band arrived and took their places next to the tree. Just then, Bonnie's mom appeared. Her paws were full with the flower garlands that she'd promised.

"Here you are!" she cried. "You can't dance without your garlands!"

She slipped one over Bonnie's head. It was made of golden buttercups and soft bluebells, fluffy meadowsweet and bright red

115

poppies. It looked beautiful next to

the rainbow colors of the willow

tree. The crowd cheered and

clapped as Sophie, Katie, and Polly

put their garlands on, too.

Sophie's mom arrived and

flew over to give her a big, soft hug

with her bushy tail. The she joined
Sophie's dad and Sammy, right
at the front. They were all waving
excitedly. Sophie thought she might
burst with pride!

When all the animals had
gathered on the banks of the spring,
the band played a fanfare with
their lily trumpets. Sophie, Bonnie,
Polly, and Katie carefully took hold
of the branches they'd practiced
with the day before.

Just as they were about to begin, Sophie looked up and saw the bluebird on his branch. But he wasn't blue anymore. Just like the tree, his feathers were now every color of the rainbow!

Oops, thought Sophie. But the bluebird didn't seem to mind at all. He puffed up his colorful chest proudly and began trilling his beautiful song, in harmony with the band.

Sophie took a deep breath. *Tail, behave!* she said in her head. She hoped the shooting-star dust would work.

Sophie's heart soared as she skipped around the tree, first this way, then that. Her tail didn't shake, so nobody sneezed. And it stayed in position, so it didn't get tangled up in the branches or trip her up. She was surrounded by a blur of lovely colors as the branches

119

of the willow tree swished to and fro. It reminded her of the beautiful shooting star and how it had drawn patterns so gracefully across the sky.

The crowd clapped and cheered as the four friends danced faster and faster around the tree. Sophie caught a glimpse of her mom and dad smiling, and her little brother laughing and clapping his paws in time.

And then, suddenly, it was over. All of Misty Wood cheered and clapped and drummed the ground with their paws. Sophie thought they might never stop!

At last the clapping began to die down, and the fairy animals set off to explore all the exciting things on offer at the fair. Sophie rushed over to her mom and dad to give them both a huge hug.

"We did it!" she squealed.

122

"You were fantastic!" Her dad grinned. "My little star!"

Sophie laughed. "Oh, but it was the *shooting* star that helped me!" she exclaimed, and gave her tail a little shake. She gasped. There was no rainbow-colored stardust left. Instead, a cloud of the usual silvery stardust shimmered in the air, then floated gently to the ground.

"It's all gone!" Sophie stared

at her dad. "I haven't shaken my tail since decorating the tree. I must have used it all up before the dance!" Sophie frowned. "But how did I manage to get my tail to behave if I didn't have any magical stardust left?"

Her dad patted her head with his paw. "Sometimes, all you need is to believe," he said with a smile. "You believed the stardust was going to help you—and it did.

It gave you the confidence you needed to do the dance perfectly. Now you can believe in yourself!"

"Wow—that really is magic!" Sophie gasped.

"Yes, it is," said her dad. "Now it's time you and your friends went off to enjoy the fair. You deserve it after all that hard work."

Sophie had been thinking so much about the dance, she'd almost forgotten that a whole day of

wonderful treats and surprises lay ahead.

As she fluttered off to join Katie, Bonnie, and Polly, she saw someone else flying along beside her.

"Can I come, too?" chirped the bluebird. "I want to show off my new colorful feathers."

"Of course you can!" Sophie exclaimed.

Together, Sophie and her

friends flew off toward the cobweb tent. The bluebird tweeted a cheerful tune as they went, and Sophie hummed along. She swished her tail happily and a trail of silver stardust shimmered in the sky behind them. What an exciting morning it had been! Today really *was* turning into the very best day of her life!

Turn the page for
lots of fun
Misty Wood
activities!

Help Sophie find the acorn cup of delicious honey at the center of the maze.

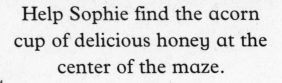

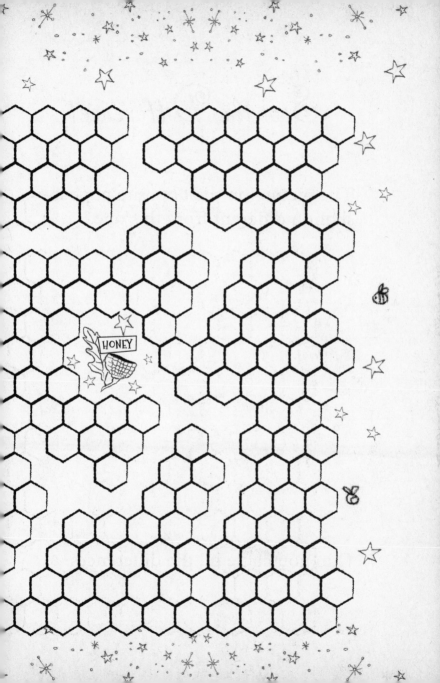

Spot the Difference!

The picture on the opposite page is slightly different from this one.

Can you circle all the differences?

Hint: There are
10 differences
in this picture!

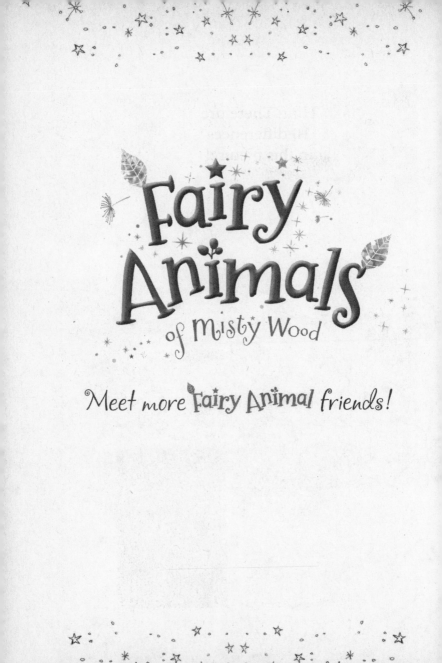

Fairy Animals
of Misty Wood

Meet more Fairy Animal friends!

Chloe the Kitten
Fairy Animals of Misty Wood
Lily Small

Bella the Bunny
Fairy Animals of Misty Wood
Lily Small

Paddy the Puppy
Fairy Animals of Misty Wood
Lily Small

Mia the Mouse
Fairy Animals of Misty Wood
Lily Small

Poppy the Pony
Fairy Animals of Misty Wood
Lily Small

Hailey the Hedgehog
Fairy Animals of Misty Wood
Lily Small

Sophie the Squirrel
Fairy Animals of Misty Wood
Lily Small

Daisy the Deer
Fairy Animals of Misty Wood
Lily Small